KILKENNY COUNTY LIBRARY

KK469494

THE

LIBRARY OF DOOM

KILLER APP

D1513138

BY MICHAEL DAHL

Illustrated by
Bradford Kendall

Raintree

www.raintreepublishers.co.uk
Visit our website to find out
more information about
Raintree books.

To order:
☎ Phone 0845 6044371
▤ Fax +44 (0) 1865 312263
🖳 Email myorders@raintreepublishers.co.uk

Customers from outside the UK please telephone +44 1865 312262

Raintree is an imprint of Capstone Global Library Limited, a company
incorporated in England and Wales having its registered office at 7 Pilgrim
Street, London, EC4V 6LB – Registered company number: 6695582

Text © Stone Arch Books 2012
First published in the United Kingdom in hardback and paperback by
Capstone Global Library Ltd in 2012
The moral rights of the proprietor have been asserted.

All rights reserved. No part of this publication may be reproduced in any
form or by any means (including photocopying or storing it in any medium
by electronic means and whether or not transiently or incidentally to
some other use of this publication) without the written permission of the
copyright owner, except in accordance with the provisions of the Copyright,
Designs and Patents Act 1988 or under the terms of a licence issued by the
Copyright Licensing Agency, Saffron House, 6–10 Kirby Street, London
EC1N 8TS (www.cla.co.uk). Applications for the copyright owner's written
permission should be addressed to the publisher.

Art Director: Kay Fraser
Graphic Designer: Hilary Wacholz
Production Specialist: Michelle Biedscheid
Originated by Capstone Global Library Ltd
Printed in and bound in China by Leo Paper Products Ltd

ISBN 978 1 406 23700 9 (paperback)
15 14 13 12 11
10 9 8 7 6 5 4 3 2 1

British Library Cataloguing in Publication Data
A full catalogue record for this book is available from the British Library.

Contents

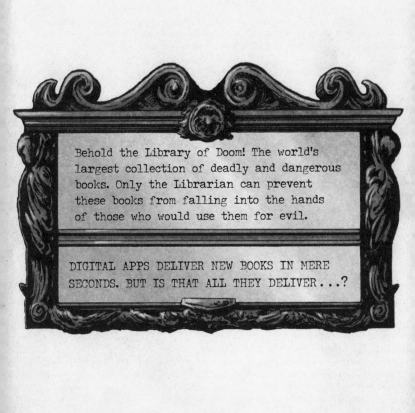

Behold the Library of Doom! The world's largest collection of deadly and dangerous books. Only the Librarian can prevent these books from falling into the hands of those who would use them for evil.

DIGITAL APPS DELIVER NEW BOOKS IN MERE SECONDS. BUT IS THAT ALL THEY DELIVER...?

Chapter 1

RAVENWING

On a quiet desert road, two black birds **FIGHT** over a piece of roadkill.

A car **flashes** by, disturbing the birds.

"This new app is killer!" says a red-haired boy inside the car.

Ivan, his best friend, and their girlfriends are **DRIVING** to a concert.

Ivan, in the back seat, stares at his phone.

"Show me, Ivan," says his girlfriend, Lauren.

Ivan holds up his phone for her to see. "The app sends me really FREAKY horror stories," he says.

He points to an ICON on the phone's screen.

The girl leans in and stares more closely at the screen.

"That looks **creepy**," she says.

Ivan laughs. "It's just a bird," he says.

KK469494

"The app is called **Ravenwing**," says Ivan. "So the icon looks like a raven's head."

"A really ANGRY raven's head," says Lauren.

"Let's see," says Bel, the girl in the front seat.

Ivan hands her his phone.

Ivan's girlfriend **shakes** her head. "Why can't you like nice stories instead of creepy horror ones?" she asks.

HA!

Both boys laugh.

HA!

HA!

Bel plays with the phone. "This is cool," she says. "Look at all the scary **STORIES** you can download. There must be hundreds of them."

"There are," says Ivan. "Go ahead, pick one."

Bel laughs. "Okay," she says. "I'll download this one. Don't worry, Lauren. It doesn't look too SCARY."

She touches the phone screen.

Mark, the driver, **GLANCES** at his rear-view mirror.

"Is a storm coming?" he asks.

The three passengers turn to look.

A black cloud is rushing towards the car.

Chapter 2

CLAWS AND TALONS

The dark cloud GROWS larger and larger. Savage screams pierce the air.

"Birds!" shouts Lauren. "It's a **giant** flock of birds!"

"This is not happening," whispers Ivan.

"Why are they **attacking** us?" cries Bel.

"Who cares?" says Lauren. "Just get the roof up!"

"It's coming! It's coming!" SHOUTS Mark.

The roof finally clicks into place. The SCREAMS of the birds grow louder.

Ivan and Lauren drop back into their seats. Another sound **rips** through the car.

Bird talons **TEAR** into the fabric roof of the car.

The teenagers scream. A sharp black beak pokes through the roof.

"Hold on!" shouts Mark.

He slams his foot down on the pedal. Tyres **screech**.

Black birds shriek.

"I don't want to be **ROADKILL**!" says Ivan.

More and more birds **ATTACK** the car.

The sky is blacked out by a mass of flapping wings.

The roof is shredded by a thousand talons.

Then . . . silence.

Two motorcycles **fly** down the road. The riders are racing each other.

The rider in the lead raises his hand. He has spotted **something** on the road ahead.

The riders, Pedro and Dave, pull their bikes to a **stop**.

KILKENNY COUNTY LIBRARY

A car sits on the road, **BLOCKING** both lanes.

Its doors are all open. Its convertible top is **shredded**.

"What's going on?" says Dave, taking off his helmet.

"It doesn't look good," says Pedro.

He climbs off his bike and walks

towards the car.

His boot **crunches** on something. He looks down.

He has stepped on a **LARGE** black feather.

Dave joins his friend next to the car.

"Whoa!" he says. "What happened here?"

The outside of the car is covered with **SCRATCHES**.

The inside is littered with hundreds of black feathers.

"Crows?" asks Dave.

"**Ravens**," says Pedro.

"What's the difference?" asks Dave.

"Ravens are **bigger**," says Pedro.
He picks up a feather and studies it.
"And they're smarter," he adds.

Dave walks to the front of the car.

"Where's the driver?" he wonders
aloud. He glances around.

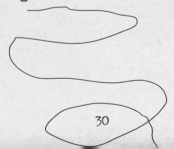

Something gleams on the tarmac.

Dave leans down and picks up an object.

"Someone's phone," he says. "We should call the police."

"We should get this car off the road," says Pedro. "The keys are right here."

Chapter 4

HORROR WINGS

Pedro turns on the engine and drives the car to the side of the road.

Dave stares at the phone screen.

"Huh," he says. "HORROR."

"What's that?" asks Pedro, CLIMBING out of the car.

"Horror," says Dave. "You know, like Stephen King, Simon Skull . . ."

"Right," says Pedro. "What about it?"

"Whoever had this phone was downloading horror stories," says Dave. "This app here. It's called **_Ravenwing_**."

"You can't download anything out here," says Pedro. "No phone MASTS, remember?"

"I know," says Dave. "But this download seems to work."

"Let's get out of here," says Pedro. "I have a bad feeling about this place. Besides, we need to call the police."

A SCREAM rips through the hot sky.

Both boys look up. A raven flaps its dark wings above the road. It circles the bikers.

A second raven joins the first. It appears out of **nowhere**.

"Hurry up!" shouts Pedro.

The boys **JUMP** on their bikes and take off down the road.

Pedro pulls in front of Dave. He spies an **old** petrol station up ahead.

Dave sees it too.

The ravens **shriek**. Their screams are almost as loud as the bikes' engines.

The two bikes swerve and turn at the last moment.

They *race* around the back of the old petrol station.

The boys quickly turn off their engines and jump from their bikes.

The ravens SWOOP down.

Dozens of birds attack the bikes.

The bikers *race* to a back door.

It is locked.

Dave throws himself against the **old** door and rams it open.

Pedro **SCREAMS**.

A raven has grabbed his leather jacket.

Dave **pushes** the bird away and yanks his friend inside the door.

Then he grabs an **old** truck tyre. He props it against the door, holding it shut.

"Are you all right?" asks Dave.

"I don't know," says Pedro. "I think so."

They **rush** further inside the station.

The cries of the ravens GROW
louder.

The bikers hear wings flapping
outside. Somewhere, glass breaks.

"They're inside!" yells Pedro.

Chapter 5

THE LAST APP

The boys find another **door**.

"Must be the office," says Pedro.

"I hope there aren't any windows," says Dave.

They push open the door and **plunge** into the dark room.

Pedro finds a light switch on the wall and **flicks** it on.

A strange woman is standing in the middle of the room.

She has long, **dark** hair. She wears boots and a uniform.

"Who are you?" asks Pedro.

The woman sees the phone in Dave's hand. "Give me that," she COMMANDS.

"But it doesn't –" Dave begins.

"Quickly. We don't have time," she says. Then she grabs the phone.

"That won't work," says Dave. He points to the phone. "There are no phone MASTS around here."

The woman smiles **grimly**. "This will work," she says.

The woman taps the phone's screen several times. "We need a new app," she says. "One that gets rid of those birds."

The air **EXPLODES** with the
screams of ravens.

Dave and Pedro brace themselves
against the door.

On the other side, the *ravens*
attack. They throw their bodies against
the door.

Sharp beaks **DIG** into the wood.

The door creaks and thuds with every impact.

The woman is busy with the phone. "I hope he finds it," she says to herself.

"What are you talking about?" asks Pedro.

"Not what," she says. "WHO."

"Ah, here's the app," says the
woman. Pedro glances over her shoulder.

The woman taps an icon for
The Library of Doom.

Chapter 6

THE MASTER

The room lights up with a blue **GLOW**.

A man now stands next to the woman. He wears **dark** glasses and a long, dark coat.

"Open the door," says the man.

"Listen to him," says the woman. "He knows what to do. He's the <u>Librarian</u>."

"I've heard of him," Pedro tells Dave. "He can control books or something. He's like, their **MASTER**."

The Librarian grins. "And here's the master of ravens," he says. He holds up an **ancient** book.

"How's a book gonna help us with these crazy birds?" shouts Dave.

"The man who wrote this book harnessed the **POWER** of the birds," says the Librarian. "Now open that door."

The door bursts open. A thousand ravens flood into the room.

The Librarian holds up the **ancient** book.

A breeze begins to **flip** its pages.

Then the wind **spins** through the
small room.

One by one, the birds disappear
inside the **ancient** volume.

The deadly flock is sucked into
the book.

Then . . . SILENCE.

The Librarian snaps the covers shut. "It is done," he says.

?

"How did you do that?" asks Pedro.

"Only horror can defeat horror," says the Librarian. "It was the Master who did it."

Then he **drops** the book on a nearby table.

The boys can see the cover.

The boys walk out of the petrol station.

Outside, they find four people, sitting on the **ground** and looking confused.

"How – how did we get here?" asks a red-haired boy.

Pedro pulls the car keys from his pocket. "I think these are yours," he says.

Dave turns to the Librarian. "And you're sure those **birds** won't come back?" he asks.

"*Nevermore*," says the Librarian.

AUTHOR

Michael Dahl is the author of more than 200 books for children and young adults. He has won the AEP Distinguished Achievement Award three times for his non-fiction. His Finnegan Zwake mystery series was shortlisted twice by the Anthony and Agatha awards. He has also written the Dragonblood series. He is a featured speaker at conferences on graphic novels and high-interest books for boys.

ILLUSTRATOR

Bradford Kendall has enjoyed drawing for as long as he can remember. As a boy, he loved to read comic books and watch old monster films. He graduated from university with a BFA in Illustration. He has owned his own commercial art business since 1983, and lives with his wife, Leigh, and their two children, Lily and Stephen. They also have a cat named Hansel and a dog named Gretel.

GLOSSARY

ancient very old

app small application on a phone or computer

tarmac hard, rubbery substance used to make roads

disturbing frightening or strange

icon tiny image meant to represent something

littered strewn about; covered

master one who controls something

nevermore never again

pierce puncture or poke through

savage cruel or violent

talon bird's claw

volume book

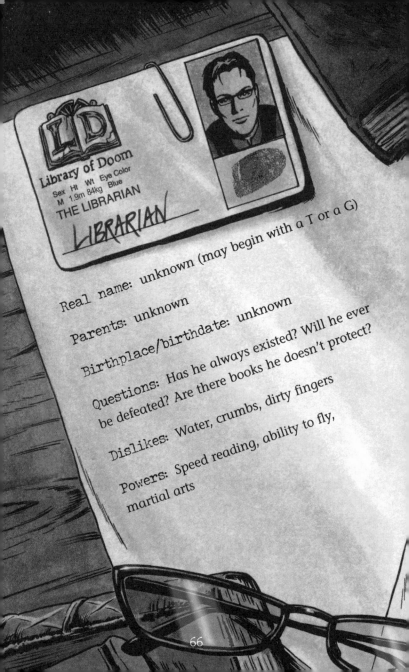

Library of Doom

Sex Ht Wt Eye Color
M 1.9m 84kg Blue

THE LIBRARIAN

LIBRARIAN

Real name: unknown (may begin with a T or a G)

Parents: unknown

Birthplace/birthdate: unknown

Questions: Has he always existed? Will he ever be defeated? Are there books he doesn't protect?

Dislikes: Water, crumbs, dirty fingers

Powers: Speed reading, ability to fly, martial arts

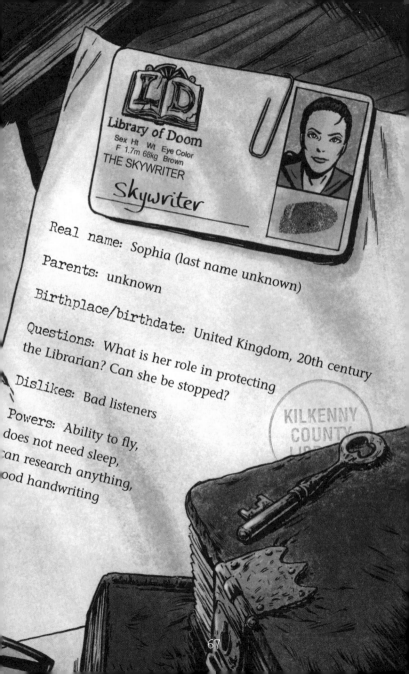

Library of Doom

Sex: F · Ht: 1.7m · Wt: 68kg · Eye Color: Brown

THE SKYWRITER

Skywriter

Real name: Sophia (last name unknown)

Parents: unknown

Birthplace/birthdate: United Kingdom, 20th century

Questions: What is her role in protecting the Librarian? Can she be stopped?

Dislikes: Bad listeners

Powers: Ability to fly, does not need sleep, can research anything, ood handwriting

KILKENNY COUNTY LIBRA

THE RAVENS

The ravens who tried to destroy the Librarian, Skywriter, and the six teenagers were conjured by the app one of the teenagers downloaded. The creator of the app is unknown. But now the Librarian knows he has another enemy, one who would turn all stories into horrific creatures, one who would use the digital world to download evil into the real world. While the Librarian's fight against this unnamed enemy has just begun, he believes all readers can help wage this war. Fight injustice with proof from history. Fight the death of imagination with the world's favourite tales. Fight drab images with poetry. It is a fight, the Librarian believes, that we all share. Our weapons are our stories. They are, after all, what make us human.

DISCUSSION QUESTIONS

1. If you had to PROTECT one book, what would
   it be? Why?

2. In small groups, talk about the Librarian. How
   did he get his job? How did Skywriter get her
   job? How do they spend their time?

3. **Edgar Allan Poe** was considered a master of
   horror. Use your library or the Internet to find
   out more about him and his stories. Share what
   you have found out in small groups. Do you
   think Poe's stories sound scary? Why?

WRITING PROMPTS

1. Create YOUR OWN APP. What does it do? What does its icon look like? Who would use it? Write about it.

2. Try writing this story from Lauren's point of view. What does that person experience?

3. Edgar Allan Poe wrote HORROR stories. Write your own horror story!

More books from the Library of Doom

Return to the Library of Doom